The Odd Couple

by

Yvonne Coppard

Illustrated by Sally Kilroy

For my niece, Katie

First published in Great Britain by Barrington Stoke Ltd
10 Belford Terrace, Edinburgh EH4 3DQ

ISBN 1-902260-65-1
Printed by Polestar AUP Aberdeen Ltd

MEET THE AUTHOR – YVONNE COPPARD

What is your favourite animal?
A cheetah
What is your favourite boy's name?
Matthew
What is your favourite girl's name?
Jessica
What is your favourite food?
Chicken
What is your favourite music?
Rock music
What is your favourite hobby?
Theatre and cinema

MEET THE ILLUSTRATOR– SALLY KILROY

What is your favourite animal?
A water-loving golden labrador called Poppy
What is your favourite boy's name?
Tom
What is your favourite girl's name?
Lucy
What is your favourite food?
Italian and Chinese
What is your favourite music?
1960s music and a saxophone
band called the Fairer Sax
What is your favourite hobby?
Playing tennis and sailing

Barrington Stoke was a famous and much-loved story-teller. He travelled from village to village carrying a lantern to light his way. He arrived as it grew dark and when the young boys and girls of the village saw the glow of his lantern, they hurried to the central meeting place. They were full of excitement and expectation, for his stories were always wonderful.

Then Barrington Stoke set down his lantern. In the flickering light the listeners were enthralled by his tales of adventure, horror and mystery. He knew exactly what they liked best and he loved telling a good story. And another. And then another. When the lantern burned low and dawn was nearly breaking, he slipped away. He was gone by morning, only to appear the next day in some other village to tell the next story.

Contents

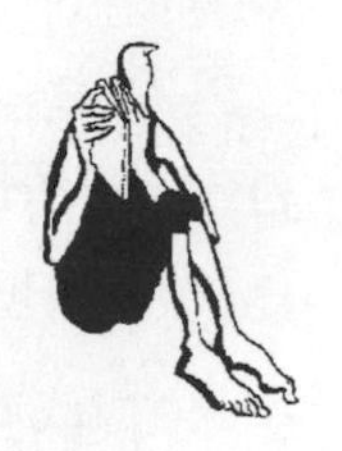

Chapter 1
Nev Knows It All

Danny knew that his neighbours were a bit strange. But he had got used to them over the years. It didn't bother him that Mr Barker never left home without putting his umbrella up. Even on fine, dry days, he would look up at the sky and shake his head. Then he would "tut tut" and put up his umbrella before setting off down the street.

Then there was Miss Smith. She lived three doors down from Danny. She was devoted to her cat, Tibbles. But she was also a very modest old lady. Once, Danny popped in to see her with some scones from his Mum. He found the cat wearing a blindfold made from a huge handkerchief.

Miss Smith cheerfully told Danny that she had just had a bath. She explained that she always blindfolded Tibbles when she undressed. "He's a male cat, you know," she said, nodding her head as if she was saying something very wise.

Next door to Miss Smith, Mr Patel had a garden gnome perched on each corner of his bath. He had shown them to Danny once. Each one had a fishing rod that dangled in the water. Mr Patel said he liked a bit of company in the bath. And the gnomes were no trouble to look after. "Not like Miss Smith's blasted cat," he muttered,

“who is always after milk and leaves dead mice on my doorstep.”

“I wish I lived in your street. Your neighbours are totally mad, man,” said Nev.

Nev was Danny’s best friend. He had been the new boy at school not long ago. He

and Danny hit it off straight away. They liked the same things, supported the same team. Nev laughed at Danny's jokes and not many people did that.

Nev came from a little village right out in the country. "If you knocked your knee, it was big news," he told Danny. "It was really boring. But there's loads of stuff going on here. And your street is brilliant. It's so full of weird people."

Nev loved weird people. He was going to be a film director one day. He was always coming up with ideas for stories. He would only have to look at someone and he could weave a story around them straight away. For instance, he told Danny he was sure their French teacher had a thing going with the man who taught them Geography.

"You only have to watch the way they look at each other," he told Danny. "Misty eyes across a crowded room – just like the girly romance films."

"Don't be daft!" said Danny. But he started watching them just the same. Sure enough, they did seem to smile and talk in a special way when they were together. That was the thing about Nev and his stories. He told them so well, you ended up believing them even if you didn't want to.

For someone like Nev, Danny's street was a great place to be. There was always someone doing something strange. Nev kept asking Danny what he thought about all the things he had discovered about the neighbours. Danny just shrugged and said, "I've never really thought about it." To him, these things were ordinary.

But Danny did tell Nev about the Tanners who lived across the road. Later he would see that this was one of the biggest mistakes of his life, but he knew Nev would love the Tanners. Even Danny found them a bit weird.

For a start, you never saw the Tanners together. They didn't even leave the house through the same door. Mr Tanner always used the front entrance, Mrs Tanner came from round the back. Mr Tanner did not appear during the day. He was only seen at night. But Mrs Tanner was in and out of the house a lot. She often wore a huge, black cloak that went all the way to the ground. Sometimes, she wore a wig. She had lots of them. She could be blonde, dark or ginger. She even had a blue wig and a silver one.

From Danny's bedroom you could see right into the Tanner's front room. There was a shop window dummy there. It moved around from day to day, as if it was alive. Sometimes it was sitting in an armchair, sometimes standing by the window as if it

was watching the street. The dummy changed clothes and hats a lot. They were often brightly coloured and in all sorts of weird styles. Sometimes the dummy looked like a man, sometimes like a woman.

When Danny told Nev about the Tanners, Nev was quite excited. He came straight over after school and peered through Danny's window from behind the curtain while Danny repeated all the odd things he could remember seeing the Tanners do.

"Don't you see?" said Nev finally. "It's quite clear." He sat back with that knowing look, waiting for Danny to get it. But Danny didn't get it.

"All right, I give in," said Danny. "What's quite clear? I know that the Tanners are fruit cakes. But what else?"

"Mr and Mrs Tanner are the same person," said Nev. "That's why you never see them together. Mr Tanner must be some kind of master criminal. During the day he dresses up like a woman to fool everyone. All he has to do is to get people to believe that he has a wife. He makes sure that only she is seen going out and about by the neighbours. And hey! They think he's at home all day."

"You sound as nutty as they are," scoffed Danny. But Nev was very convincing once he got going.

"Think about it. You never see both Tanners together. You can't even see their shape, under those loose, black clothes. And why do they wear wigs? And what's the dummy for? Well, the dummy can be dressed up and put in a chair or sat at the table all cosy and part of the family. Any suspicious policeman keeping an eye on him will think it's Mr Tanner. But it's just the dummy, of course. Meanwhile, Mr Tanner slips out dressed as *Mrs* Tanner and goes about his robberies, or whatever he does, right under the cop's nose."

"That kind of thing happens in films, not real life," said Danny. "I admit they do look very like each other. That's spooky for a married couple. OK, I might even be able to accept that Mr and *Mrs* Tanner are just one person. But if Mr Tanner is a master criminal, why live here in Barnfield Road? He can't be very good at robberies if he has to live in an ordinary house like that."

"Honestly, Danny, you are so thick sometimes," said Nev. "Where better to live without anyone noticing you than a street like this? No one takes much notice of who comes and goes. The dosh is all hidden away somewhere. One day, when he has stashed away enough, he'll be off to live in another country – lots of sun, sea and champagne and no one ever able to get him for his crimes."

The more he thought about it and the more he spied on the Tanner house, the more convinced Danny was that what Nev said was true.

Danny quizzed Nev again. "So when he goes out, you reckon it's to do a crime? Is that just when he's being Mr Tanner, or is it in the daytime when he's dressed up as *Mrs* Tanner as well?"

"There's only one way to find out," said Nev. "We set up watch and follow him!"

Chapter 2
Danny And Nev Go Spying

Over the next few weeks Nev and Danny spent as much time as they could watching the Tanner house. They dashed home from school, or got up early on Saturday, to start watching. They told their parents they were working on a homework project that they needed to do together. Their parents were very impressed.

"Nice to see you making an effort at last," said Danny's Dad.

"It's about time you got down to your school work," said Nev's Mum.

Most of the time Danny and Nev sat doing nothing. They just peered at the Tanner windows and kept watch. As soon as it started to get dark the curtains were drawn and they couldn't see anything any more. But when Mr or *Mrs* Tanner went out, Danny and Nev went out too.

"Nev may as well move in with us," grumbled Danny's Mum. "Why can't you go to his house for a change?" She also grumbled about the way they left the house suddenly, grabbing their coats and dashing out of the door. "Where's the fire?" she shouted after them.

They didn't get so many chances to follow Mr Tanner, because it was always late in the evening when he went out. But they managed it a couple of times. He went to the riverside docks area of the city, where there were a lot of run-down pubs and clubs. He knocked at the heavy door of The Blue Snooze night club. Someone let him in. Danny and Nev waited outside for a long time but he never came out. In the end they had to go home.

"The Blue Snooze must be where his headquarters are," said Nev. "Maybe he meets up with his gang to plan the jobs and decide who will do what on the night."

When Mr Tanner was dressed up as *Mrs* Tanner, she was much easier to follow. Danny and Nev got quite good at hopping on and off buses without being seen.

Mrs Tanner went all over the place. Often she carried a large, black leather bag. Usually she ended up at a big house, or a hired hall. She would go in, stay for anything between half an hour and a couple of hours and come out again. Danny got very bored with watching and waiting, but Nev passed the time telling Danny all the ideas he had about what was going on inside.

"If it's a big job, there will be alarm systems to knock out and a safe to crack," he said with glee. "Or maybe he's had to tie someone up while he gets on with it. We're dealing with a very clever criminal here, no doubt about it."

Nev sounded just like Danny's Grandad with that last bit. Danny would have laughed if he didn't feel so sick. His stomach was churning over and over. When he thought of Mr Tanner robbing someone, he always imagined an empty house.

But what if someone did walk in on him? Would he really tie someone up, like they did on television? Whatever crime it was, it had to be something nasty. Why else would Mr Tanner only go out at night, or pretend to be a woman when he went out by day? He must be very worried about being caught.

Chapter 3
We Have To Get The Proof!

Danny could not work out what was going on, but he was worried. "We must tell someone," he said. "This is too big for us, Nev. It could be dangerous. Maybe we should go to the police."

"You have got to be joking," said Nev. "Who will believe us? We need proper proof before we do anything. The police will just laugh at us."

“I suppose you’re right,” said Danny.

All the same, Danny tried to talk to his Mum. He didn’t tell her he and Nev were following Mr and *Mrs* Tanner. But he told her about the weird clothes and the dummy in the window. “Nev’s idea is that there is only really one person in the Tanner house. He says …”

"I might have known Nev started this off. That boy has an amazing imagination," said Danny's Mum. "The Tanners keep themselves to themselves and that's their right. Mr Tanner may well like to dress in women's clothes. So what? It's none of our business. Live and let live, I say. So leave the poor man alone. And just don't let this game of yours get out of hand, Danny."

"It's not a game, Mum. Someone might get hurt ..." But Mum was singing along to the radio while she peeled the potatoes. She nodded at him, but she wasn't listening. Nev was right. They had to get more proof.

Danny and Nev carried on watching and following the Tanners for the next two months. Then one Saturday Danny noticed that the dummy had been dressed in a black hat and cloak. And it was wearing a mask over its face. It looked quite terrifying. He called Nev.

"Get round here, quick. I think something big is going to happen."

Sure enough, as it began to grow dark there was activity in the Tanner house. Mr Tanner, dressed as a woman, came in to the front room and took the hat and cloak and mask from the dummy. Then he drew the curtains and they could see no more. But a few minutes later, Nev and Danny saw *Mrs* Tanner coming up the path from the back of the house.

"This is it, Danny," said Nev. "The big one!"

Chapter 4
Mr Tanner Makes A Move

Mr Tanner walked quickly, wrapped in the cloak. He was carrying a large, black leather bag. He got on a bus. Danny and Nev got on just as it pulled away.

"Where to?" asked the driver.

"I don't know," said Danny.

"We're just ... bus spotting," said Nev. "Give us a ticket for the end of the line."

The driver raised his eyebrows, but said nothing. Like Danny, he had grown up in the city and was used to weird people.

Mr Tanner got off the bus two stops later and the boys jumped off too.

"You kids today have money to burn," said the driver. "This bus goes on for miles before it reaches the end of the line. You could have walked the two stops to get here."

Danny wondered what the driver would say if they told him they were following an evil criminal.

Mr Tanner got on another bus. Danny and Nev followed him. This time he stayed on for three stops. When he got off, he walked quickly down a busy main road. Once or twice he looked back over his shoulder as if he had seen them. They

ducked into shop doorways. Mr Tanner didn't challenge them, so they thought they must have got away with it.

A few minutes later they turned into a long, leafy avenue with big houses and very private-looking gardens. Mr Tanner stopped at one of them. He paused at the gate and looked all around. The boys turned their backs and pretended to be looking at a map so he couldn't see their faces.

Mr Tanner did not go up to the front door of the house. He went down the path that led to a side door and knocked three times.

The door was opened by a tall, well-built man with very short hair. "Donna!" he boomed. "We're ready for you. Come on in."

"So that's what Mr Tanner calls himself by day. Donna!" said Nev.

"Donna?" echoed Danny. "That's not a very robber-like name, is it?"

"It's all part of his cover," hissed Nev. "He's an ordinary woman until he's safely inside and then ... Dan, we have to get in and see what's going on."

"Yeah? And how do we do that?" asked Danny. "I don't know about you but I have no experience in breaking and entering."

He hoped it wouldn't be possible to get in. His stomach was churning and he could feel his heart starting to thump about. He didn't want proof of what Tanner was up to any more. He just wanted to go home.

Nev tried to calm Danny down. "I'm not saying we should do anything criminal, Danny. But we can't just go and ask him what he's up to, can we? We'll have to think of a good trick. Come on." Nev started creeping through the bushes that lined the path to the side door.

"Nev, what are you doing? Come back!"

Nev took no notice. Danny couldn't leave him, not if there was danger. He made himself follow Nev up the path.

Chapter 5
Getting Into Danger

Danny and Nev were almost at the door when they heard someone talking in the street. They crouched down in the bushes and waited.

Two women and a man came up the path, laughing and joking. "He won't know what's hit him," said one of them.

"Sssh," said the man. "We don't want him to know we're here." He knocked on the door three times, just like Mr Tanner. It was opened by the same man who had let Mr Tanner in.

"We're with Donna," said one of the women and they went into the house.

"I wonder why they aren't using the front door," said Nev. "Do you think they are planning to do something to the owner? Maybe he knows too much, or he just doesn't want to be involved any more. Either way, he has to be dealt with."

Danny's stomach turned over again. "You don't think they'll hurt him, do you?"

"Or worse," said Nev.

"Nev, we'd better go. Robbery is dangerous enough, but what if Mr Tanner is a murderer? Let's just get home and tell ... Nev, what are you doing?"

Nev marched up to the door and knocked – three times. Terrified, Danny came to stand beside him. The door opened. They had done it now.

Chapter 6
An Odd Instruction

"Yes?" The man who answered the door looked even bigger and more threatening close up.

"Er, we're with Donna," said Nev. His voice squeaked at the end.

The man looked suspicious. "You're a bit young for all this, aren't you?"

"Just part of the game," said Nev, quick as a flash. "We're a lot older than we look. Two boys wandering around doesn't attract attention."

"Well, you've done a great job. You certainly fooled me. You only look about fifteen. Come on in, I'm Reg."

The house was almost completely dark. Here and there candles flickered in small, glass pots. There was a spicy smell in the air.

"Get ready to run when I shout," whispered Nev as they followed the man down the dark hallway.

Reg turned round. "Sssh. We're not supposed to be here, remember?"

Reg opened a door and led them into a small room. It was some kind of cloakroom.

There was a washbasin and a large mirror. A string of white fairy lights hung around the frame. Against a wall, next to another door, there was a clothes rail with two ballgowns and a long, black cloak. Beside the rail, on a chair, were two diamond tiaras and two white sticks. There were also two long, curly wigs. One was gold and one was silver.

"You'd better get changed," said the man. "You're on soon."

"Changed?" said Danny. He looked at the ballgowns. One was pink, one white. Both had sparkly tops full of sequins and a full-length skirt with lots of net and more sequins. Danny looked at Nev and saw the same horror in his eyes.

Nev still managed to keep his wits about him though. "Oh, put on those ballgowns, you mean," he said.

The man narrowed his eyes. "Donna has told you what's expected, hasn't she?"

Nev laughed. There was still a bit of a squeak in his voice. "Well, you know Donna," he said.

Reg sighed. "She's deeply dippy. If she wasn't so good at what she does ... well, it's the fairy princess routine for this one. Right?"

"Oh, fine. No problem," said Nev, his eyes still on the costumes.

Reg pointed at the door by the rail. "When that door opens, that's your cue. Go through there and do your stuff. I'll leave you to it." He looked at his watch. "But you'd better hurry. Donna will be starting in a couple of minutes. Now I'm going to lock the door, in case you-know-who tries to get in. We haven't done all this preparation to be discovered now, at the last minute."

"Do you really need to lock us ..." started Danny nervously. But Reg had gone.

"And who on earth is 'you-know-who'?" Nev added in a whisper.

The key turned in the lock. They were trapped.

Chapter 7
Fairies?

"Nev, you got us into this mess. What did you think you were doing, banging on the door? Now they'll find us out for sure. We've had it, Nev. And it's all your fault!"

"Calm down," said Nev. "Don't panic. I'll think of something. Meanwhile, all we can do is play along and look for a way out." Nev grabbed the white dress and started to take off his shirt and jeans.

"I hope you're joking," said Danny. "No way am I wearing that stuff."

Nev threw the pink dress to Danny. "Our lives might be in danger here. We have no idea what they're up to. Until we do, we just have to go along with them. Now stop messing about and get the ballgown on. When that door opens, we must look as though we know what we're doing, at least for a few moments. If I see any way at all that we can get out, I'll give you a signal. I'll shout, or tap your arm, or something. First chance we get, we leg it. We stick together, play along and hope to God whoever is through that door is so surprised to see us that we get a chance to run."

Two minutes later they stared at each other in horror. The dresses were not quite large enough across the back, but they gaped at the front where the bosom should be. The diamond tiaras slid about and knocked the wigs into a slant. Danny tried to steady his with the hand that wasn't holding the fairy wand. Beneath the puffy net skirts their trainers looked even more scruffy than usual.

"Kick them off," said Nev. "They're a dead give-away."

Finally the boys stood in full costume. Only their socks and underpants were their own.

"I'm scared," said Danny. "I want to get out, right now. Let's see if we can pick the lock."

He crouched down, in his frock, by the locked door. "Have you got a hairpin, Nev?"

"Don't be daft," hissed Nev.

Danny heard a noise outside. "Someone's coming ..." he hissed back.

He heard the man's booming voice. "The little liars. I thought there was something odd about them. I'll deal with them – you get ready."

"They're on to us," gasped Danny.

The key went into the lock.

"Quick – that's our only chance," said Danny, pointing at the other door. He flung it open and shoved Nev through it. Then Danny stumbled and fell against Nev. They both went flying onto the floor.

Chapter 8

They Are On To Us!

There was a roar of laughter as Nev and Danny fell over. The boys sat up. At first, they were blinded by brilliant lights. Then they saw that they were on some kind of stage. In the darkness beyond the stage they could see figures sitting on chairs like an audience. The room was full of people. Nev and Danny squinted their eyes against the lights. They couldn't see any of the

people in the room clearly. They were just large, dark shadows.

But they could see Donna, dressed in a black ballgown. Donna was on the other side of the stage, staring at them with an open mouth.

The laughter went on for some time. The boys helped each other up and looked around with wild eyes for some sort of escape.

"What, foul sisters?" Donna suddenly said, stepping forward. "Have you followed me here to spoil my evil scheme?"

"Er, too right, we have," said Nev.

"Yeah – as soon as we find out what it is!" added Danny.

The audience laughed again. Donna came over to Danny and Nev and spoke to

them in a very low voice. “Get ready to dance across to the other side of the stage when I wave my wand. There’s an exit.”

The awful truth began to dawn on the boys. But it was too late. They had stumbled into a play of some sort.

Donna stood in the middle of the stage in the flowing, black cloak, carrying a mask. The look on Donna's face meant she was furious. The boys were spoiling her show.

She spoke again, this time in a loud voice. "Not so fast, sisters. You have indeed led me a merry dance, but you will dance to your graves for all I care. Dance, dance away." Donna screamed with laughter, a real witchy cackle.

The boys stood staring at her. They were confused and frozen to the spot. They didn't know what to do. The audience roared with laughter. They thought it was all part of the show.

"You are under my spell. Dance on!" Donna cackled again and then said to the boys in a loud stage whisper, "Dance across there and get the hell off my stage!"

Danny led the way, trying to remember what his sister did in her Christmas ballet show. Nev gripped his arm and tried to follow him. It was slow going with Nev's weight dragging him back. Much to the delight of the audience he slipped and fell a couple of times. Nev came tumbling down on top of Danny and let slip a few mild swear words. But finally Danny managed to get them both off the stage and out through yet another door.

Reg was waiting for them. "Right, you two," he said. He grabbed each boy by the arm and thrust them into a room across the hallway. He slammed the door and stood against it. There was no way out.

"You've got some explaining to do," he said.

"It's like this," started Danny nervously.

"Not now!" interrupted Reg. "Save it for when Donna comes." He leaned against the door in moody silence, staring at them.

Chapter 9
The Final Blow

Danny and Nev seemed to wait forever. Danny shifted his feet and coughed. He wanted to catch Nev's eye to see what ideas he had. After all, Nev had promised to get them out of this. But Nev studied his shoes, the carpet – anything to avoid eye contact.

Danny realised Nev had no idea how they could escape. Whatever strange things Donna and these other people were planning to do, Danny and Nev were going to have to watch. If it was something nasty, they were going to be the witnesses who knew too much and had to be killed off so they couldn't talk. Danny thought of the canal and the cement works just a few streets away and shuddered.

Donna burst through the door. "Who the hell are you and what the hell do you think you are doing?"

Close to, you could see she was a real woman, with a woman's body and a woman's voice. And she was hopping mad.

Behind her, staring at them in complete surprise, was a man dressed in an old-fashioned velvet suit and cloak, with a golden crown on his head.

Beside him were two beautiful, teenage girls. One wore a long, gold and white dress tied at the waist with a red sash. The other wore a black dress like Donna's and the same kind of pointy hat.

Danny and Nev looked again at the man and they both gasped aloud. A new wave of horror swept over both of them. They knew him! It was none other than Mr James, their headmaster from school! Danny closed his eyes and started praying that Mr James would not recognise them with the wigs and dresses on.

"Just a minute," said Mr James. "I think I recognise these lads. Take those wigs off."

Danny and Nev looked at each other. They didn't know what to think. They couldn't move. Their own headmaster, involved in a gang of criminals. He would certainly not let them live to tell the tale.

"You haven't gone shy on us, surely," sneered Donna. She ripped off the wigs. The tiaras fell to the floor.

Now it was Mr James's turn to gasp. "Daniel and Neville! What on earth are you doing here?" he demanded to know.

"Aren't you the boy from the family who lives opposite me?" said Donna. "I told my brother you were spying on us a couple of weeks ago. He didn't believe me."

"Your ... your brother?" Nev's voice was not much more than a whisper.

"My twin brother, yes. He runs the business with me."

"What business?" asked Danny.

The girls were trying not to laugh, but could not stop themselves. Danny caught sight of himself in the mirror – full fairy dress with his closely cropped hair with Wallace and Gromit socks poking out from underneath all the net skirts. He must look a real sight. He felt his cheeks burning and knew this made him look even worse.

"Tanner Entertainments," said Donna. "We do night clubs, children's parties, singing telegrams ... you name it, we'll entertain you. Now tell me, why are you here?"

"We thought ... we thought you ..." Danny was completely put off by the giggling girls. He could not think of a way to make it sound at all sensible. He was beginning to get the idea that he and Nev had made real fools of themselves. He just wasn't sure exactly how they had managed it.

Nev, however, had recovered his form. "Actually," he said calmly, "we have been investigating you. We know all about your business. Fishy business," he said, waving his arm in a way Danny thought he had seen a famous TV detective do it. "We were suspicious of the way you and your so-called brother are never seen together. You never leave the house by the same door as each other. And what about the mystery dummy that moves around and changes its clothes? And I have never seen Mr James wearing a suit like that to school ..."

Nev felt Mr James stare at him and spluttered to a halt. Mr James looked very angry. But Donna suddenly started to laugh. The two girls joined in and didn't seem to be able to stop. The boys got redder and redder.

Finally, Donna said, "I just hope you two don't want to be detectives when you grow up."

"Grow up? That day's a long way off," giggled one of the girls.

"Let me explain," said Donna. "You don't deserve an explanation but I'll give you one. The fact is, my brother and I have half the house each. So we each have our own front door. Mine is round the back of the house. The front room is the office and workroom. We design and make costumes there. It's the only part of the house that's shared. So you should have been able to see both of us together in that room at least sometimes. You didn't snoop hard enough. We do go out together sometimes too, I promise you. Not that it's any of your business."

"I don't believe this," said Mr James angrily. "You boys have been spying on a neighbour, following innocent people going about their business. On top of that, you get into my house under false pretences and spoil my birthday party ..."

"Your what?" Nev groaned. "Oh no … don't tell me all this is just a fancy dress party."

"You guys are in big trouble," said the girl in black. "I don't know what you thought was going on here, or why you came without being invited. But what you see is my Dad's surprise 50th birthday party. He loves pantomime. So my sister and I hired Donna to arrange one that he could take part in at the last minute with no rehearsal. We were doing *Sleeping Beauty*, with Dad as the father. Your costumes were for the good fairies. Two dancers Donna hired showed up a bit late. Meanwhile, looks like Reg thought you must be part of the comedy turn and gave you the costumes."

"You have spoiled the whole thing," said Donna crossly.

"Oh, I don't know," said Mr James. "They had a certain stage presence. I'll remember you when it comes to school show time. You look very fetching in pink, Daniel. I wish I had a camera handy so that I could snap you for the school noticeboard."

"They do look very cute," giggled one of the girls. "Tell you what, Dad, I'll go and get my camera. Don't go away, little fairies."

Nev scowled and Danny's face got as red as it was possible to get.

"Look, we're really sorry," said Danny. "We got it all wrong. But we didn't mean any harm. We'll just get out of your way now and let you enjoy the rest of the celebrations. Happy Birthday, Sir."

The boys started edging towards the door. Reg stepped in front of them. "Not so fast."

“*Please*, can we go?” pleaded Danny.

“Photograph first, I think. It will be a useful reminder to you when I need volunteers for things at school.” Mr James raised the camera his daughter had brought to him. “Smile, please.”

He clicked the camera three or four times, with everyone smirking and giggling in the background.

"Right, you are free to go. Reg, will you show them to the front door?"

"Um, we just need to collect our clothes first," said Danny.

Mr James smiled grimly. "Oh no you don't. You have wandered around my house long enough. You leave right now, or I'll call the police and tell them we have a couple of trespassers."

"You wouldn't do that!" gasped Nev.

"He would," said Danny, who had known Mr James a lot longer than Nev.

"But how will we get home? We can't go out looking like this. Besides, our money is in our jeans," wailed Nev.

Carefully, Mr James counted out some coins from his pocket and handed them to Danny. "I think you'll find there's just enough there for the bus," he said. "But not for a taxi, even if they would pick you up looking like that, so don't bother trying. Come to my office in school on Monday morning and I will return all your belongings and take back the costumes. And they had better be in excellent condition, so treat them carefully on your journey home."

Nev could not believe Mr James really meant to send them home wearing fairy frocks. "Come on, Sir. We know we did wrong. We really are sorry. Put us in everlasting detention or something. But you can't make us go home looking like this. Not on the bus. What will people think?"

"They will think you are a couple of stupid and immature idiots, I expect," said Mr James. "And they'll be right. Now, off you go. I'll see you Monday."

Before they knew it, Danny and Nev had been marched down the hall and out of the front door. As it slammed behind them they heard gales of laughter.

There was nothing for it but to board first one bus and then another in their silly fairy costumes. Even before they reached the first bus stop, Nev and Danny were cold and tired. Their feet were wet and their socks were ruined. There would be no way either of them could sneak into the house unnoticed. They knew there would be big trouble waiting for them at home when they tried to explain what they had been up to.

People pointed and stared and laughed at them all the way home. One old lady thought they were collecting for charity and tried to give them money. Worse still, a group of boys from their own class saw them. It would be all round school on Monday.

"Nev, I am never going to listen to you again," said Danny as they sat on the second bus with the driver giving them a long, hard stare. A young mother gathered her children close. "You and your imagination. You really had me convinced. I'm never going to believe your crazy stories again ... Nev, are you listening to me?"

Nev turned to his friend with that sparkle in his eye that Danny knew so well.

"Sorry, Dan, didn't catch what you said. But listen." Nev lowered his voice. "Don't look now, but see that man three seats down facing us? That bulge in his left pocket is a gun, I'm sure it is ..."

"Oh, Nev!" sighed Danny.

Barrington Stoke would like to thank all its readers for commenting on the manuscript before publication and in particular:

Jason Bechtle
Maddy Brook
Rosa Brook
Beatrice Brook-Farrell
Elliott Brook-Farrell
Alison Coughtrie
Millie Gillingwater
Rosalind Hall
Isabella Holmes
Katherine Howe
Gillian Reeve
John Shaw
Annie Younger

Barrington Stoke Club

Would you like to become a member of our club? Children who write to us with their views become members of our club and special advisors to the company. They also have the chance to act as editors on future manuscripts. Contact us at the address or website below – we'd love to hear from you!

Barrington Stoke, 10 Belford Terrace, Edinburgh EH4 3DQ
Tel: 0131 315 4933 Fax: 0131 315 4934
E-mail: barringtonstoke@cs.com
Website: www.barringtonstoke.co.uk

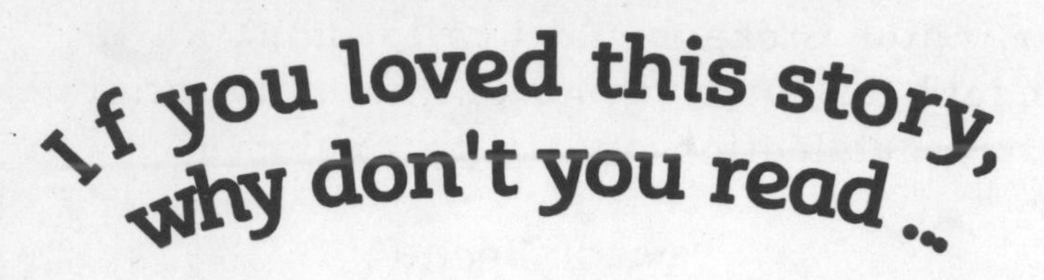

No Accident

by Lesley Howarth

What would you do if everything that happened to you was your fault? If you let your dog eat your watch? Let yourself be bullied at the bus stop? Or let yourself meet somebody who changes your life completely?